D1106669

BOG
HOLLOW
BOYS

Bog Hollow Boys is published by
Stone Arch Books, a Capstone Imprint
1710 Roe Crest Drive
North Mankato, Minnesota 56003
www.mycapstone.com

Library of Congress Cataloging-in-Publication Data
is available at the Library of Congress website.

ISBN: 978-1-4965-4058-4 (reinforced library bound)
ISBN: 978-1-4965-4062-1 (eBook PDF)

Summary:

Someone's messing with the buzzards at Bog Hollow State Park.
Luckily, the Bog Hollow Boys are on the case.

Designer: Ted Williams
Editor: Nate LeBoutillier

Printed and bound in Canada.
010010S17

GONE TO THE BUZZARDS

BY C.B. JONES

STONE ARCH BOOKS
a capstone imprint

TABLE OF CONTENTS

The **BOG HOLLOW BOYS** vow to protect, serve, and nurture the animals in and around Bog Hollow State Park (B.H.S.P.). No animal is too small, large, cute, ugly, slimy, furry, feathered, stinky, or dirty for their attention. Bog Hollow Boys to the rescue!

AUSTIN "ACE" FINCH
Age: 12
Skills: leadership, grit, birds

NELLIE TIBBITS
Age: 12
Skills: smarts, sass, snakes

DARYL "DA SNAKE" TATE
Age: 12
Skills: jokes, wrestling, pets

ETHAN "EL GATOR" FINCH
Age: 10
Skills: tagging along, wrestling, fish

RANGER FINCH

Father of Austin and Ethan and the warden of B.H.S.P.

DR. TIBBITS

Mother of new girl Nellie and famous herpetologist

MS. FINCH

Mother of Austin and Ethan, P.E. teacher, & wrestling coach

MISS DENISE

Granny of Daryl Tate, lover of cats, & outstanding cook

THE MANLEYS

Bad boy brothers who are always up to no good

WILLIE AND BUD

B.H.S.P. deputy rangers who keep a watchful eye on the park

CHAPTER ONE

SCAVENGERS OF DEATH

The Bog Hollow Boys were out picking trash along Copperhead Trail. Austin Finch had his sights set on a crushed Coke can a few feet away. He liked to imagine himself a spear fisher from olden times. He took a deep breath and closed one eye. Over his shoulder he cradled the long stick he'd whittled into a trash spear.

Leaves rustled behind him. Austin looked back and saw his little brother Ethan crawling with his chest an inch off the ground. He had stuffed his trash picker down his shirt. The pinchers stuck out in front of his face like alligator jaws. The little weirdo was crazy for alligators. He really liked to call himself "El Gator." Austin just usually called him Gator Bait.

Ethan was about to jump out at Daryl Tate, the third member of the Bog Hollow Boys. Daryl wasn't a Finch brother, but he might as well have been. All three of them spent their time solving cases along the swamps and bogs of South Georgia. Around those parts, there was always some case to solve.

Daryl lagged behind as usual. He had taken off his big floppy straw hat to use like a flyswatter. "Get off me, you dang dirty gnats!" he said. He flapped the hat. A floral-patterned strip of cloth wrapped around the hat's crown came loose.

Austin and Ethan both knew it was Daryl's grandma's gardening hat. But Daryl would never admit this.

"You know who you're messing with?" Daryl said. He was talking to the gnats.

Ethan was ready to pounce. He and Daryl were always wrestling. Daryl was two years older, but he was no bigger or stronger than Ethan.

"You're messing with Daryl Da Snake Tate, that's who," said Daryl. He swung wildly at the gnats and lost his balance. He rolled backward, stumbling right into Ethan.

They tussled in the dirt and leaves. For a second there, it really did look like a snake and an alligator wrestling. When they made it to their feet, they started circling each other.

Daryl hissed.

Ethan made chomping noises.

"You stepped on Da Snake's tail one too many times, Gator Bait," Daryl said.

"That's El Gator to you, Snake Face!" Ethan spit back at Daryl.

"Who you calling Snake Face, Gator Bait?"

This went on for a while. Names were called. Threats were made. Austin rolled his eyes but stayed out of it. He was focused on the three big black birds circling up above them.

"Shh . . ." Austin whispered. He glared at Daryl, then Ethan. He pointed toward the sky. "Turkey vultures," he said. "Scavengers of death."

Daryl and Ethan forgot about wrestling.

"*Scavengers of death,*" Daryl whispered in a spooky voice. He couldn't take his eyes off the circling birds.

Ethan said it, too. "*Scavengers of death.*"

"What do you think they're hunting, Ace?" Daryl asked. He had called Austin "Ace" since the very first time they met, back in kindergarten. Austin never really understood why, but he liked it.

"They're not hunting anything," Austin said. "They're scavengers. They only prey on dead stuff."

"Well, Mr. Smarty Pants," Daryl said, "what do you think died?"

"I'd sure like to go find out," said Austin. "Wouldn't you?"

"Sounds like a case for the Bog Hollow Boys to me," Daryl said.

"What do ya say, Gator Bait?" Austin asked. "You think you're ready for whatever mystery Bog Hollow has to offer us today?"

"Chomp, chomp," Ethan said, clapping his gator arms. "El Gator was born ready, boys."

CHAPTER TWO

POOR
BUZZARD

They tracked the vultures all the way out to an old dirt road just off park property. Ethan and Daryl stood in the middle of the road, bent over and wheezing.

"This snake ain't cut out for all this heat," Daryl said. "Snakes are *cold* blooded. Don't you fellas know that?"

"So are gators!" Ethan said.

Austin wasn't listening. He was busy surveying the scene. He spotted a dead armadillo belly up along the shoulder of the road. Its scaly little claws stuck straight up into the air like exclamation points: *Dead! Dead! Dead! Dead!*

Then there were the vultures. Three of them fought over different parts of the armadillo they'd they plucked out.

It didn't take long before Austin noticed a fourth vulture laying there motionless further up the road.

Austin snuck up for a closer look. The other vultures hissed and flapped their wings a little but didn't fly away. They kept on eating. If they were mourning their fallen friend, they sure didn't show it.

When Ethan came up and caught a look the buzzard's head, he froze. All he could say was, "Whoa."

Daryl noticed, too. "Whoa," he said.

Big fat tire tracks ran right across its red featherless head. They also ran across its limp wings. Scattered feathers danced in the wind.

"Who do you think ran him over?" Ethan said, a slight crack in his voice.

"Them ain't truck tires. That's for sure," Daryl said. "What do you think, Ace? ATVs?"

Austin could feel hot tears welling up in his eyes. But he couldn't look away. "I think something's fishy," he said. "That's what I think."

Daryl pinched his nose and shook his head. "That ain't fish, Ace. That's some stinky rotten armadillo."

Austin didn't respond. He'd spotted something floating down in the drainage ditch and headed straight for it.

Daryl and Ethan stood and watched from the road as Austin made his way toward the old culvert. They still hadn't budged by the time Austin crawled back out covered in moss, muddy water, and cobwebs.

He handed Daryl a yellow trucker hat. A bulging arm muscle flexed on the logo. Above it read, *MANLEY CONSTRUCTION*. Underneath it read, *The Right MAN For the Job*. Then Austin pointed down the road.

A big yellow sign towered in front of the tree line. It had an even bigger bulging bicep painted on it. It also read *MANLEY CONSTRUCTION*.

"Quite a coincidence, don't ya think?" Austin said. "The Manleys building a new fishing pond out here. Hobie and Hunter Manley out racing around the back roads with their four-wheelers. And now this vulture with a fresh set ATV tracks running across its head."

"Poor Vinnie," Ethan said. "He didn't stand a chance."

"Vinnie?" Daryl asked.

"Vinnie the Vulture," Ethan said. "The least we can do is give him a proper name."

Daryl shook his fist. "It ain't right," he said. "The Manleys went too far this time. They went and ran over poor Vinny here."

"This stinks," Ethan said.

"Oh, it stinks, all right," Austin said. "It stinks like another Manley mess."

"For Vinnie!" Ethan said putting out his fist.

"And for Arnie!" Daryl thrusting his fist out, too.

Both Ethan and Austin cocked their eyebrows at him. "Arnie?" Austin asked.

"Arnie!" Daryl said pointing back at the armadillo getting slowly dissected by the three remaining vultures. "Even stinky armadillos deserve justice."

"Fine," Austin said. "For Vinnie *and* Arnie."

CHAPTER THREE

THE RANGER'S WARNING

Dusk had blanketed Bog Hollow. Austin told Daryl and Ethan to sit tight outside the ranger station. He'd talk to the warden alone first.

Bud and Willie sat outside the warden's office. They fidgeted, drumming fingers and bouncing feet. They were deputy rangers but looked more like a couple kids waiting to see the principal.

Bud was short and stout and wore a too-small plaid shirt. His meaty arms dangled from the short sleeves. "I wouldn't go in there if I was you," he told Austin.

Willie shook his head. "Boss ain't a happy camper today, boys." Willie was tall and lanky and looked like a lizard. "Guess who dumped a whole can of gas in the swamp this afternoon?" He jerked a thumb at Bud.

"On accident," Bud said. "Anyway, it's not like Captain Genius here helped much. He got his four-wheeler stuck and ran out of gas spinning his wheels. Burned about three gallons of gas like that." Bud snapped his fingers.

"You didn't run over any animals, did you?" Austin asked.

"Course not!" Willie said. "You know I'd never—"

Austin had been holding the doorknob when the warden suddenly yanked the door open.

Ranger Finch was a good six feet tall. He towered extra tall with his ranger hat. "Y'all figured out how you're gonna clean up our swamp yet?" he asked Bud and Willie.

Then he noticed Austin. "Were y'all out there picking trash this whole time?" he asked. "Your mama's gonna chew both our butts if I get you home late for dinner."

"Something bad happened, Daddy," Austin blurted out. "Somebody ran over a vulture out on the back roads." Austin explained about the hat and the sign. He explained about the four-wheeler tracks and how the Manleys were always racing around out there

22

with their four-wheelers. He explained that they weren't even old enough to be riding alone!

"It was Hunter and Hobie," Austin told his dad. "I know they did it. They killed an innocent bird."

Ranger Finch let out a big sigh. "Innocent vulture, huh?" he said. He turned to Bud and Willie. "Looks like you fellas just pulled roadkill duty," he said.

Bud and Willie didn't say anything. They nodded and grabbed their flashlights.

As they headed out the door the warden called after them. "Let's try not to poison any more of our wildlife this time, you two clowns."

On the ride home that night, Austin's dad said he didn't want to hear any more. He made Austin promise to stop going around starting things with the Manley boys. He also made Austin promise not to tell his mom about the dead vulture.

Austin and Ethan's parents had been divorced for almost three years now. According to their mom, their dad loved the Bog Hollow State Park more than he'd ever loved her.

The truck rolled to a stop out in front of her house. Daryl and Ethan said goodnight, hopped out, and headed in. Austin remained in the cab.

"You can't fill your mama's head with all these wild stories," the warden said. "You hear me, Austin?" He looked Austin straight in the eyes. "If your mama thinks I'm putting y'all in danger out at the park, that will be the end of your adventures."

Austin picked up the ranger hat resting on the bench seat between them. He traced the felt brim with his fingers. "I promise, Daddy," he said.

"Okay," said the warden. "Go on, then."

Austin said goodnight and got out of the truck. On his way in the house, he whispered to himself, "I promise never to let Mama stop me from standing guard over Bog Hollow."

CHAPTER FOUR

SHOW AND TELL

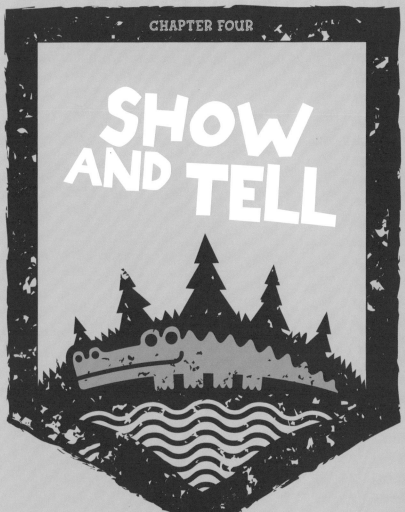

It was Friday morning in Miss DeLoach's classroom at Eagle Creek Middle School and that meant Show and Tell.

Daryl went first. "And what will you be showing us this morning, Daryl?" Miss DeLoach asked.

"Well Miss D," he said, "this morning I wanted to introduce y'all to a couple friends of mine." Daryl quickly slipped off his shirt before the teacher could stop him. "This one's Larry," he said and slapped his left bicep. Then he slapped his right bicep. "This one's Roger."

Every morning Daryl took a black marker and drew a snake on each arm. He flexed and tried to make the snakes dance as best he could. Then he started to demonstrate his patented sleeper hold on an invisible opponent.

"Young man," said Miss DeLoach. "This isn't a professional rasslin' arena." She led him back to his desk by the arm.

"Da Snake may be stifled," Daryl whispered to Austin. "But he'll never be silenced." He hissed with each S sound.

Austin ignored him. He twirled three vulture feathers between his fingers.

Miss DeLoach told the class to take out their science books.

"But Miss DeLoach," Austin said, holding up his feathers. "I didn't get my turn."

Miss DeLoach sighed. "Haven't you already shown us your feathers, Austin?"

"No ma'am," Austin said. "Not these ones."

Miss DeLoach wagged her finger. "No funny business, mister."

Austin passed two feathers out to the classroom. He held the third high for everyone to see. It was almost eight inches long.

"Can anybody identify this feather?" Austin asked.

Austin did not call on Daryl, but Daryl answered anyway. "Them's buzzard feathers, Ace."

Austin narrowed his eyes at Daryl. "Actually, these are the feathers of the North American turkey vulture."

"Exactly," Daryl said. "Turkey buzzard."

"No," Austin said. "You can call it buzzard or you can call it turkey vulture, but you can't call it turkey buzzard, Daryl. Well, I mean, you can. But it's wrong."

Austin went on to explain that turkey vultures were strictly scavengers. "They don't kill other animals," he emphasized. "They feed off fresh roadkill, mostly."

"That ain't true," Hunter Manley blurted out from the back. He and his twin brother Hobie were pale and freckle-faced with matching towheaded mullets.

Miss DeLoach cleared her throat. "Hunter Manley," she said. "You will raise your hand in this class."

"Fine," Hunter said. He raised his hand and kept talking. "Me and Hobie see buzzards kill armadillos all the time."

"Yeah," Hobie said. "And them dirty buzzards probably got our cat, too. We ain't seen Fat Bertha in a week or so."

Austin let out a sigh. "I'm sorry about your cat," he said. "But turkey vultures only go after roadkill. And the roadkill around here is usually stray cats and armadillos."

"Sure, but let me ask you this," Hunter said. "How do you think they end up roadkill in the first place?"

Austin wanted more than anything to point his feather at them and shout. But he'd promised his dad.

"Well they ain't bein' killed by vultures," Austin said, his voice rising. He paused for a second. "Who knows?" he said with a shrug. "Maybe somebody's out there runnin' down innocent animals with their unlicensed four-wheelers?"

Of course, Hunter wasn't listening anymore. Someone had passed him a feather. He was tickling Hobie's ear. Hobie giggled as he ran his hand through the blond shock of his mullet.

Austin grit his teeth and looked around the room. No one was paying attention. *It's all a big joke to the Manleys*, Austin told himself. They were making a mockery of a feather from the very bird they had run over and killed.

Miss DeLoach asked Austin if he had anything else to share about vultures.

"Yeah," he told Miss DeLoach. "One more question. Do y'all know how vultures stay cool when they're out in the sun all day?"

No one said anything. They were still distracted by the Hunter and Hobie show. Austin raised his voice. "They poo on themselves!"

"Ew!" someone squealed again. It was Hobie. He squirmed up out of his desk and stumbled backward.

Hunter dropped the feather like it was a pair of stinky undies. He puckered up his face and made ralphing noises.

Austin didn't blink. A small grin came across his face. It was the first time Austin had smiled since he'd found poor Vinnie run over.

CHAPTER FIVE

THE HERPETOLOGIST'S DAUGHTER

That Saturday the boys all headed back out to Bog Hollow to finish their garbage duties. They were grabbing trash pickers when Ranger Finch drove up on his mule.

A woman rode next to him. She had a bright red streak in her dark hair and thick black-framed glasses.

The girl riding in back looked even stranger. Her bright red hair was pointing straight up. She'd shaved the sides, spiked the top, and dyed the tips purple. The idea that it brought to mind was that of a Mohawk on fire.

"Morning boys," Ranger Finch said. "Let me introduce our new neighbors."

The woman came over to introduce herself. She pushed her thick glasses up into her hair and held out her hand. "Dr. Evie Tibbits," she said.

It was hard for Austin to focus on shaking with that girl's head on fire. Ethan's mouth was actually hanging open as he looked at the girl's Mohawk. Daryl had to elbow him to shut it.

"Dr. Tibbits here's a professor of herpetology," Ranger Finch said.

"Her-puh-what?" Daryl blurted out.

"Herpetology!" the Mohawk girl shouted. "We study reptiles," she said. "Especially snakes. *Poisonous* snakes!" Every word sounded like a bottle rocket shot straight through her pointy nose.

Dr. Tibbits shushed her. "Nellie," she said. "Come over and properly introduce yourself."

The girl didn't budge.

"You'll have to excuse my daughter," Dr. Tibbits said. "We just moved all the way down here from the state of Wisconsin. Might take her a while for her to let her guard down."

"Y'all might as well hurry up and learn to get along," Ranger Finch said. "Nellie and Dr. Tibbits are gonna be spending a lot of time here helping us track our venomous snakes."

Both Austin and Nellie groaned.

Austin's dad stared straight at Austin. "So let's show Nellie here some proper Southern hospitality."

Daryl stepped up first. "I'm Daryl Da Snake Tate," he said. "But you can just call me Da Snake if you want. See I'm a bit of a snake-ologist like y'all.

"You mean herpetologist?" Nellie asked.

"Yeah, exactly," Daryl said, "You wanna meet some other snakes?"

"Keep your shirt on, Daryl," Austin scolded.

"Why don't y'all grab Nellie an extra trash picker," Ranger Finch told them. "Dr. Tibbits and I are gonna check out some snake holes. See what we can stir up."

As the adults took off, Daryl started in. "Welcome to Bog Holler State Park, Nellie," he said. This here's Ethan and Austin Finch. Around these parts people call us the Bog Hollow Boys."

Nellie said, "*Who* calls you that?"

"People who know what's what," Austin said.

Nellie shook her head. With those spikes, she looked like a rhino ready to gore anything in her way.

Daryl stepped between them. "What Ace here means, Nellie, is that we're dedicated to preserving the wildlife around here," he explained. "Right, Ace?"

"Just keep in mind it's the Bog Hollow *Boys*," Austin told her.

Nellie kept wrinkling up her nose and pawing the ground with her foot. She'd dug a clear line in the dirt between her and Austin.

Daryl slowly backed away from both of them. As he walked past, he whispered, "Da Snake would tread real carefully, Ace." He nodded at the Nellie, whose face was starting to match her hair.

"It's okay, D," Austin said loud enough for Nellie to hear. "She can tag along on trash duty if she wants. The Bog Hollow Boys are always happy to welcome new helpers. What do ya say, Nellie?"

She still hadn't looked up, so he waved his hand to get her attention. "I mean unless you think it'll be too scary out there in the swamps."

She pawed the dirt one last time and then let out a short unsteady breath. When she looked up, her face had slack. She put her hands to her cheeks. "But what if I see a *big . . . scary . . . spider*?" she said. Each word she said was spit from her mouth. She held out her hand as if to shake and then pulled it back.

Whiff!

Austin's hand dangled in the wind as she marched past him. He still had his hand out when Daryl walked up, grinning.

"I told ya, Ace. I done told you," he whispered in Austin's ear. "I'd tread carefully with this one."

"Daylight's wasting, boys," Nellie called back to them. She already had twenty yards on them and Austin's trash spear over her shoulder. "And we've got trails to blaze."

CHAPTER SIX

TROUBLE AT DINNER

A couple nights later, Austin and Ethan were at their mom's house for dinner. She had them cleaning shrimp. They'd already shucked the corn and cut up the potatoes for their mama's specialty: low country boil.

She'd invited their new neighbors over for dinner.

"But Mama . . . " Austin said. "Have you seen Nellie's hairdo? And also, she, like, sleeps with snakes or somethin'. She's weird."

"Around here, son, we welcome all newcomers," his mom said. She was slicing pieces of sausage. "Besides," she continued, "she can't be any weirder than Daryl. And we've basically adopted that boy."

The doorbell rang, and Ms. Finch said to grab the door. Ethan bounded across the den to the front door. Austin sulked at the table.

Ethan had a big goofy grin as he swung the door open. "Welcome to our humble abode," he said.

"Why, thank you, good sir," Dr. Tibbits said.

Nellie's posture mirrored Austin's slouch. Her shoulders were slumped as she stared at her shoes. Neither said a word.

Ethan giggled and made a grand sweeping motion with his arm toward the kitchen. "Come right this way, miladies."

At dinner, Austin put his head down and tried not to make eye contact. He shoveled forkfuls of shrimp, corn, potatoes, and sausage.

Nellie put her head down, too, but didn't eat. She squinted and sniffed at a pile of potatoes and corn piled on her plate. She'd already lined up all the shrimp and sausage alone one side of her plate.

"My apologies," Ms. Finch said. "If I'd known y'all were vegetarians, I would've made extra corn and taters."

Dr. Tibbits smiled and took another nibble of potatoes. "These are just wonderful," she said. "Aren't they, Nellie?"

Nellie took a bite of potato and swallowed hard. "Mm-hmm," she said. "Wonderful."

Dr. Tibbits changed the subject. "So, Austin. Your dad tells me you've been having vulture troubles."

"Your daddy got you boys out there messing with dangerous animals again?" Ms. Finch snapped.

"No ma'am," said Austin.

"Turkey vultures aren't really dangerous," Dr. Tibbits said. "They're just scavengers."

Ms. Finch turned to Dr. Tibbits. She was smiling, but Austin and Ethan saw that their mama's eyes were dark, the way they were when she was mad and trying not to show it.

"No offense, Dr. Tibbits," their mom said. "But I know my boys and I know my ex-husband. They'd lose an eye if it meant saving a buzzard from stubbing its beak."

The table went silent. After a long and drawn out moment, the quiet sounds of chewing and clinking forks slowly resumed.

Ms. Finch speared a slice of sausage on the end of her knife. She eyed it like a starving hawk might eye a wounded rabbit.

It was Nellie who broke the silence. "It's not these two I'd necessarily be worried about, Ms. Finch," she said. "From what Daryl says, it's those two Manley boys."

"Who's that?" Dr. Tibbits asked.

"Just a couple of neighborhood knuckleheads," Ms. Finch said. She turned her glare to Austin and Ethan and said, "I thought we were done with all of this foolishness."

"Y'all ever wrestle up there in Wisconsin?" Ms. Finch asked. She was pointing her steak knife at Nellie. "And I'm not talking about fake rasslin' neither. The real thing."

"No, ma'am," Nellie said. "Nothing organized."

"Why don't you come down to the gym after school on Monday," Miss Finch said. "Austin and Ethan, too. I'll teach all y'all a thing or two about dealing with knuckleheads." Then she added, "*Without* getting in trouble."

Dr. Tibbits frowned, but Nellie saluted and said, "Sign me up, Coach."

Nellie smirked as Austin sat there slack-jawed with a mouth half full of shrimp and potatoes.

"Careful, Ace," she said. "Don't choke before we even get to wrestle."

CHAPTER SEVEN

TIME TO WRESTLE

Austin and Ethan's mom had been the first female wrestler from Eagle Creek ever to go All-State. Now as the gym teacher at the boys' school, she displayed her medals and trophies in her office.

"Know what those are?" Ms. Finch asked Nellie that Monday. "They're a testament to what you can accomplish in this life if you make sure to not listen to stupid boys."

Austin sat in the corner sketching in his notebook. He was drawing a flock of vultures circling the heads of two pudgy little boys.

Daryl was trying to demonstrate his patented sleeper hold on Ethan. "First Larry here slithers up under your chin," Daryl told Ethan as he put him in a headlock. "And while you're fighting off Larry, old Roger here cinches it in around the back, here."

As he always did, squirrely little Ethan slipped Daryl's hold and squirmed free. "El Gator escapes again!" he declared.

"Dang it, Gator Bait," Daryl said. "How are you ever gonna learn to rassle if you can't hold still?"

"Y'all rassle like two little girls," Hunter said with big smirk. "Yeah," Hobie echoed. "Like two little girly girls."

"Ain't y'all supposed to be on detention scrubbing toilets somewhere?" Austin said. He dropped his notepad.

Before either Manley could think of a comeback, Austin's mom came marching out of her office. Nellie followed, her arms full of headgear and uniforms.

"I invited them," Miss Finch said. "I thought we could end all this name-calling and learn to handle things face to face on the wrestling mat."

When Nellie handed Hunter his uniform, he bunched it up in his fist. "Uh-uh," Hunter said shaking his balled up uniform. "I ain't wrestling no girl."

"Me neither," Hobie said. "Especially not in this." He held up his uniform with two fingers as if he'd just caught a mouse in his underwear drawer.

Austin hated to say it, but he was with Hunter and Hobie. "It ain't right, Mama," Austin said. "She might get injured."

"That so?" Miss Finch said. She had her arms crossed and a stony expression on her face. Nellie stood next to her, mirroring her pose.

"How about you two?" she asked Daryl and Ethan. "Y'all afraid of a girl too?"

"Sounds to me like these boys are scared, Coach," Nellie said. She cupped her ear for a moment and listened. "I think I can hear their knees knocking."

"I ain't afraid of no girl!" Hunter said.

"Me neither!" Hobie said.

"If she wants to wrestle," Austin said, "I'll teach her to wrestle."

"It's settled then," Miss Finch said. "Now get ready to get your hurt on."

For the next hour, Miss Finch put them through drills and lectured them about proper technique. She spent much of the time lecturing Daryl that the sleeper hold was not a legal wrestling maneuver. She spent equal time yelling at Hobie and Hunter to suck it up and show some hustle.

By the time they got to grappling, they were all breathing heavy. Miss Finch had Austin and Nellie come to the middle to demonstrate the basics.

Miss Finch told Austin to face Nellie in starting position. Then she showed him how to grab Nellie by the insides of her elbows.

"This is what they call the inside hooks," Ms. Finch explained. "If Austin here gets his hooks in tight, Nellie won't be able to do much of anything."

Austin said, "You hear that? When I get the hooks in, you won't be able to do nothin'."

"We'll see about that," Nellie said back.

"Just try it," he said. He gripped her elbows as hard as he could. "I dare you."

In one swift move, she slipped out of his grasp and dropped flat on her back. As Austin reached out to grab hold, he lost his balance. Before he knew it, Austin lay face down with Nellie on his back, wrenching his arms behind his shoulders.

"How's that for you?" she asked.

Austin didn't talk. His face was smashed into the mat. He heard the Manleys snickering and Ethan giggling. He heard it loud and clear.

"Take it easy now, Nellie," his mama was saying. "Don't injure the boy."

"I told you, Ace," Daryl was saying. "I done told you. You gotta watch out for that snake girl. She got some fangs on her."

CHAPTER EIGHT

HISSING
AND BARKING

That weekend the Bog Hollow crew was back looking for clues on the road where everything had started.

They'd just come across another armadillo when they heard barking coming from up the road by the Manleys' place.

"*Shh*," Austin whispered. "I think I hear Bubba, the Manleys' bulldog."

By the time they heard the four-wheelers, Austin had already taken off. Nellie took off a split second later. Neither looked back.

Nellie caught up with Austin twenty yards from the Manley's driveway. "Now where do you think you're headed?" Nellie said.

"I've got some unfinished business," Austin said. "Just stay out of my way,"

"How's this for staying out of your way?" She darted across the ditch. Her skinny legs were a blur as she vanished into the woods.

Austin turned down the driveway and saw Bubba. The Manleys' bulldog was bouncing and barking at something or another.

It was a vulture. The bird's feathers were ruffled up. Its wings were spread wide. But its talons were dug deep into something furry and it wasn't about to give it up. Austin threw himself right between the hissing vulture and the snarling bulldog.

"Bad Bubba!" Austin shouted. "Go home, Bubba!"

As the words left Austin's lips, the Manleys appeared, gunning their four-wheelers straight for him.

Hunter got within ten feet when he slammed on the brakes. He skidded another ten feet towards Austin, Bubba, and the bird. Hobie nearly flipped his four-wheeler on top of himself trying the same move.

"This bird ain't done nothin' to y'all!" Austin shouted. "He's just trying to survive."

Hunter pointed his stubby finger at Austin. "That there bird done killed our kitty cat." His voice cracked a little as he spoke.

"That ain't your cat," Austin said. "That's a possum, genius. Can't you see its bony claws? Besides, I told y'all. This bird only eats what's already dead."

Hunter said, "I'm gonna count to three. Then you best be running." He smacked his pudgy fist into the palm of his doughy hand. So did Hobie.

"Go ahead and hit me," Austin said. He closed his eyes and braced for the punch. "I'm not gonna let y'all kill another innocent vulture."

Hunter counted to three. Nothing happened. Not to Austin, anyway. A thunk resonated, and Hobie cried out like a dying cat. Another thunk resounded, and Hunter yelped. Austin opened his eyes to see both of them holding their heads. They'd ducked for cover behind their four-wheelers. Bubba was running back home as fast as his little legs would take him.

A hissing noise came down from behind him. Austin looked, but the vulture had gone back to work on the possum as if nothing had happened.

"This ain't over, Finchy," Hunter called out as he hopped on his four-wheeler. "We'll see how tough you are at the wrestling tournament next weekend."

"Yeah," said Hobie.

As the Manleys zoomed away, Austin again heard the hissing sound. He spun just in time to duck out of the way of a whizzing acorn. When he looked up, he saw Nellie perched in the crook of an old scrub oak.

"Ssss . . . ssss," she said. She smirked and tossed an acorn up and caught it.

CHAPTER NINE

TOURNEY TIME

Ten other kids entered the first annual Eagle Creek Junior Wrestling Tournament. That made sixteen with Miss Finch's wrestlers.

There were two weight classes. Hobie, Hunter, and Austin were thrown in with the hundred-pounders. Daryl, Ethan, and Nellie were all under a hundred.

Daryl wrestled first. He also lost first. Ranger Willie was reffing and he warned him twice that the sleeper hold was illegal. The third time Daryl tried to choke out his opponent, Willie had to disqualify him.

Ethan lost in the first round, too, and it didn't take very long. He'd started with his alligator arms routine, circling his opponent and sizing him up as he planned out his attack.

While Ethan circled, his opponent snagged him in a Fireman's Carry. Five seconds later he was pinned.

Nellie, on the other hand, breezed through to the lightweight finals. She hadn't been pinned all day. She didn't even have to take them down. They took themselves down trying to catch her.

Word spread quickly about the girl outwrestling all the boys. The crowd roared when Nellie took to the mat for the championship. Her opponent, Chandler Stringer of Mossy Oak, was long and spidery and had at least three inches on her.

"Go get 'em, Nellie!" Daryl shouted. "Give that boy the fangs."

"Yeah, Nellie!" Ethan shouted. "Bite that boy. Bite him hard."

Austin glared at them. "Traitors," he muttered.

Then Austin caught sight of his father in the bleachers. *He was sitting with Nellie's mom!*

Austin shook his head. He looked to see if his mom had noticed. "Mama will put an end to this funny business," he told himself. But Miss Finch was too busy giving Nellie a pep talk.

"Cut that boy down to size," Austin's daddy yelled.

Everyone has turned against me, Austin decided. *And they've taken Nellie's side!* His face burned with hot tears. Without a word to anyone, he stormed off before anyone could see him cry.

He had his own match to think about anyway. He'd be wrestling Hunter in the finals. "The real championship," Austin muttered to himself. "The big boys."

Daryl and Ethan were still talking about Nellie when Austin came around looking for them after Nellie's match.

"You should've seen Nellie," Daryl said.

"She won the lightweights title, Ace," Ethan said.

"I told you, Ace," Daryl said. "I done told you she's got them—"

"Don't say it," Austin said.

But Daryl said it anyway, "—*fangs*!"

"Enough about Nellie, okay?" Austin said. He tried not to lose his temper. "Listen up, guys. Y'all wanna teach those Manley boys a lesson?"

He squatted on the mat and laid out the plan. "We'll make those Manleys some extra-special sports drink for their win," Austin said.

"What about Nellie?" Daryl asked.

She was over posing for a picture for the school newspaper. Austin's mom posed with her arm around her. On the other side, Willie raised her hand in victory and pointed at the medal hanging around her neck.

Dr. Tibbits and Ranger Finch stood off to the side beaming big smiles. Austin's dad looked as if his own kid had just won.

"She's busy," Austin said sharply.

CHAPTER TEN

WRESTLERS
AND
FEATHERS

Austin delayed his match with Hunter as long as he could to give Ethan and Daryl time to put their plan in motion.

For the first two periods, Austin played matador. Every time Hunter shot for his knees, Austin would dodge and send Hunter stumbling out of bounds.

Ranger Bud was reffing this match and he'd given Austin two warnings for stalling. "Quit dancing and get to rasslin'," Bud told him. After the second warning, Bud awarded Hunter a point.

Even Austin's mom had lost her patience. "What are you doin' out there?" she asked Austin between periods. "I certainly did not raise you to wrestle like this."

"But I'm winnin' the match out there, Mama," Austin said.

It was true.

Even with the penalty, he was still up two-one. With all Austin's escapes and reversals, Hunter had yet to score a point for himself.

"Not in my book, you're not." She grabbed him by the shoulders and shook him. "Son, you can't keep running from bullies your whole life. You gotta knock 'em on their butts sooner or later."

"Hey!" Hunter said.

Miss Finch shushed him. "Hold your horses," she said. "I'll be over tell you what you're doing wrong in a minute."

She told Hunter to suck it up and quit lollygagging. "Just squish him already!" She was looking straight at Austin. "Look at him. Look how scared he is."

The buzzer sounded for the final period. Austin caught sight of Daryl and Ethan in the doorway to the gym. Daryl gave Austin the thumbs up. Nellie was with them.

"Why the heck is she here?" Austin mouthed. He was still focused on Nellie when Bud started the period. He didn't see Hunter shoot for his legs and slam him on his back.

Hunter smothered him against the mat. Austin felt like he was drowning. Under all that sweaty flesh, he heard Hunter grunting. He heard his mom yelling at him to slip out. He heard Bud slap the floor and start counting.

The next thing Austin heard was the crowd applauding. He slumped over as Bud raised Hunter's arm in victory.

Hobie pointed and laughed at Austin on the way to congratulate his brother. Hobie and Hunter were giving each other high fives as the photographer snapped photo after photo for the school newspaper.

They didn't even notice Nellie, Ethan, and Daryl lugging over the water cooler behind them.

Nellie let out a long shrill shout. "*Yee-haw, boys!*" she said. She laid on a Southern accent as thick as the concoction they were about to dump on the Manleys. "Y'all done smooshed Ace just like ya did that vulture!"

It was quite the concoction that Ethan, Daryl, and Nellie dumped on the Manleys' little celebration. They had mixed up three parts cherry sports drink with one part molasses in a big sports drink cooler.

Then just for good measure, they'd stirred in a healthy heaping of Austin's collection of feathers.

"Ew . . . gross!" Hobie squealed.

"Stop squealing and get this off me," Hunter shouted at his brother. They shook and shook their arms, but the feathers stayed stuck.

The photographer let out a little giggle at the sight of them but kept on snapping pictures.

"This one's for you, Vinnie," Austin whispered to himself. "And for Arnie too." He wasn't sure the Manleys had run over the armadillo, but he was sure that they'd done enough damage in their lifetimes to deserve whatever blame they got.

"Can somebody please tell me what's going on here?" Ranger Finch finally said.

Hobie and Hunter were howling as Miss Finch rubbed their eyes with the towel. She cleared just a little bit so that they could see, but their blond eyelashes were still stuck together. Their mullets were pasted to their fat heads.

Austin smiled and pulled a feather from Hobie's shoulder. He pointed at the photographer, then back at the Manleys. He winked at Nellie and the boys. "I can see the headlines now. Can't you?"

"What do you say, boys?" he said, pointing the feather at them. "Are y'all gonna finally confess how you killed that innocent vulture? Or do you need another bird bath, courtesy of the Bog Hollow Boys?"

ABOUT THE AUTHOR

C.B. Jones is a transplanted Southerner who came from the Northern Great Lakes area. When not teaching collegiate writing courses, Jones spends time writing love poems and adventure novels, feeding the dog, and setting bone-crushing picks in pick-up basketball games. Other amusements include Civil War artifact hunting, spelunking, and checkers.

ABOUT THE ILLUSTRATOR

Chris Green is an Australian artist known for creating quirky characters. He has a strong love for bad jokes, great coffee, and all things related to beards. When he isn't illustrating for film or print, you might find him re-inventing the wheel with his 3D printer, playing with power tools in the shed, binge-watching television shows, or spending time with his lovely wife and their wonderful circle of friends.

GLOSSARY

ABODE — the place where someone lives

COINCIDENCE — something that happens accidentally at the same time as something else

HERPETOLOGY — a branch of zoology dealing with reptiles and amphibians

KNUCKLEHEAD — a stupid person

MANEUVER — a planned and controlled movement that requires practiced skills

MULLET — a hairstyle in which the hair is cut short in the front and sides and left long in the back

PRESERVE — to protect something so that it stays in its original condition

SCAVENGER — an animal that feeds on whatever it can find

TOWHEADED — the presence of light blond or tousled hair

TURKEY VULTURES

Be careful where you play dead. If you lie still on the ground in the middle of a forest, a field, or a garbage dump, a turkey vulture might mistake you for carrion. Carrion is the rotting flesh of animals that have passed on. To a turkey vulture, which may also be called a buzzard in North America, carrion makes a delicious snack!

With an average wingspan of five to six feet, turkey vultures are big birds. Some people mistake them for hawks or eagles. But turkey vultures raise into a V pattern when airborne, and their flight pattern is wobbly. If you get a look at the bird's head, you won't be confused. The one that looks like a it was dipped in lava is a turkey vulture's. Bright red and scorched-looking, it's not the prettiest thing you've ever seen.

TURKEY VULTURE FACTS

→ Vultures don't have vocal cords, so they can only hiss or grunt.

→ Turkey vultures and black vultures are very similar, although turkey vultures have bright red heads.

→ To stay cool, turkey and black vultures will often urinate or defecate down their legs.

→ Vultures are excellent at flying and using air currents to stay in the air without much effort.

→ Orville and Wilbur Wright observed turkey vultures to understand the principles of flight, which helped them fly the first airplane in 1903.

→ Turkey vultures almost never kill prey. Instead, they eat recently killed animals. They are instrumental in helping keep our roads clear of roadkill.

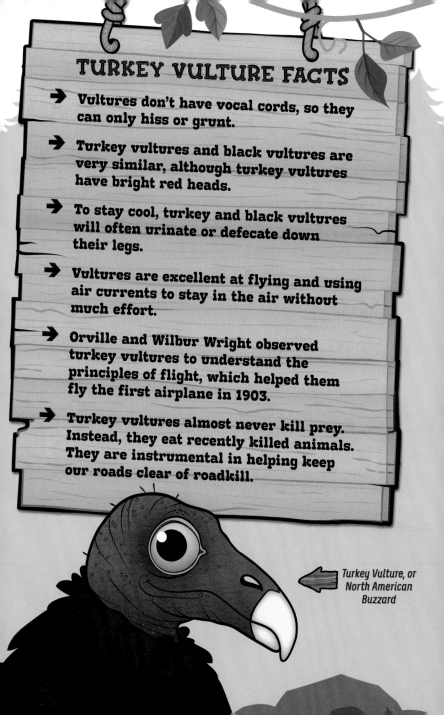

Turkey Vulture, or North American Buzzard

THE ADVENTURE DOESN'T STOP HERE!

READ ALL THE BOG HOLLOW BOYS BOOKS AND FOLLOW THE MISCHIEF!

DISCOVER MORE AT
WWW.CAPSTONEKIDS.COM